In memory of my dad, Jack, who always
made this time of year magical —S.L.

For Brigitte & Werner —M.L.

ISBN 978-1-339-03238-2

Text copyright © 2021 by Suzanne Lang. Cover art and interior illustrations
copyright © 2021 by Max Lang. All rights reserved. Published by Scholastic Inc.,
557 Broadway, New York, NY 10012, by arrangement with Random House
Children's Books, a division of Penguin Random House LLC. GRUMPY MONKEY
is a registered trademark of Pick & Flick Pictures, Inc. SCHOLASTIC and
associated logos are trademarks and/or registered trademarks of Scholastic Inc.

The publisher does not have any control over and does not assume any responsibility
for author or third-party websites or their content.

12 11 10 9 8 7 6 5 4 3 2 1          23 24 25 26 27 28
Printed in the U.S.A.                                40

First Scholastic printing, September 2023

Book design by Nicole Gastonguay

The text of this book is set in Bernhard Gothic.

# GRUMPY MONKEY
## OH, NO! CHRISTMAS

By Suzanne Lang

Illustrated by Max Lang

SCHOLASTIC INC.

**I**t was a grizzly, drizzly December day, just as it had been all week. Jim Panzee wasn't in the mood to celebrate. "Can't it be nice for one stinking day?" Jim sighed, and set out into the wet in search of breakfast.

But when he finally found a banana, it was green. "Figures," said Jim as he tossed the banana aside.

"Are you gonna eat this?"
asked his neighbor Norman.
   "No," said Jim. "It's not ripe!"

"It'll ripen in your
stomach," said Norman.

"You didn't even peel it!"
Jim said.
   "The peel's where all the
vitamins are," said Norman.

"I don't think that's true," said
Water Buffalo from beneath the tree.

"Who cares if it's true?" said Oxpecker. "It's
almost Christmas, and everyone knows green
bananas are much more Christmassy than
yellow ones. Because green is a Christmas
color! I'M SO EXCITED FOR CHRISTMAS!"

"The weather stinks! The bananas stink!
What's there to celebrate when everything
stinks?!" snapped Jim.

"Nothing to celebrate?!"
Oxpecker couldn't believe it.
"But it's such a magical time
of year! There are presents!
And visiting relatives! And
decorations!"

"Oh, no, not decorations . . . ," said
Water Buffalo.

"Of course decorations!" chirped
Oxpecker as she wrapped some berries
around Water Buffalo's horns. "Decorations
help spread Christmas cheer! See, Jim,
don't you feel like celebrating now?"

"No!" said Jim, and he stomped away.

Jim was so busy stomping, he didn't notice Marabou. "Why are you stomping around, Jim?" asked Marabou. "You should celebrate. It's such a magical time of year."

"Celebrate? Me? I don't feel like celebrating!" said Jim.

"Maybe a song will help. Fa la la la la—"
"Ugh!" Jim held his ears and stomped on . . .

. . . right into a puddle of mud.

"Hooray! Jim, you're just in time to enjoy some of our holiday treats!" croaked the frogs.

"Nothing makes you want to celebrate like a little fly pot pie, am I right?" said Bullfrog.

"Celebrate?! Me?! I don't feel like celebrating!" said Jim.

Everyone wanted Jim to enjoy this magical time of year.

"You should wrap presents!"

"And put them under a tree!"

"You should make a card for your mom!"

"You should take a long winter's nap!"

"Don't forget your dad!"

"You should light seven candles!"

"Or nine!"

"You should quietly reflect."

"You should eat sugar plums!"

"You should do something nice for someone else!"

But Jim didn't feel like doing any of that.
"Why aren't you celebrating, Jim?" asked the others.
"It's such a magical time of year."

"The bananas aren't ripe. I'm soaked and covered in mud. This fly is driving
me crazy, and you're all giving me a headache. How can I celebrate when . . . .

And he stormed off.

Jim tried to ignore all the holiday celebrations.

But he couldn't ignore the rumbling in his tummy. "Maybe Norman's right. Maybe the banana will ripen in my stomach."

He peeled a green banana and ate it.

"Ow ow ow! Norman wasn't right."

"Norman wasn't right about what?" asked Norman.

"About the bananas," said Jim. "Now my stomach hurts. And I still have a headache. And I'm muddy. And wet. And come to think of it, I'm cold too. Not to mention this fly won't leave me alone! How can anyone celebrate when everything stinks?!"

"Sounds like you could use some tea," said Norman.

"Tea?" said Jim. "I don't like tea!"

"Have you ever tried it?"
asked Norman.
"No," said Jim.
"Maybe give it a try,"
suggested Norman.

Jim took a sip of the tea.
It warmed him all the way to
his tummy. In fact, it started
to make his tummy feel better.

"It's made with mint leaves that grow right here.
Pretty nice, huh?" said Norman.

"I never noticed the mint leaves," said Jim.

"They do a good job of blending in," said Norman.

"Can I get that for you?"
said Chameleon.

"Thanks," said Jim. "I guess there are
a lot of things I haven't noticed."

"It can be hard to notice things when you've got a lot of complaints," said Norman.

Jim looked around.

He noticed how pretty the raindrops looked on the leaves.

And that the holiday tree made a pretty good umbrella.

And that he was surrounded by loved ones.

"Taking time to notice the good things can make your problems seem smaller," said Norman.

Jim agreed.

And that was a reason to celebrate.